A Stone Full of Wait

earthling k

Title: A Stone Full of Wait
Author Name: Earthling

Published by Zero Degree Publishing

Zero Degree Publishing
No.55(7), RBlock,
6th Avenue, Anna Nagar
Chennai - 600040
Website: www.zerodegreepublishing.com
E Mail id: zerodegreepublishing@gmail.com
Phone: 89250 61999

First Edition by Zero Degree Publishing:
ISBN:978-93-95233-66-8
TITLE NO ZDP: 70
Cover Design & Layout: Vidhya Velayudham

...and for all the earthlings who wait...

All matter Waits with a purpose.

This is the story of

Stone

who was filled with Wait !

and..

her friend , Wait !!

Every being is pulled into 'wait' whether it is

silly

small

reckless

smart

loving

meticulous

slow

mindful

shabby

wary

cautious

microscopic

scared

suspicious

funny

rational

or even mysterious!

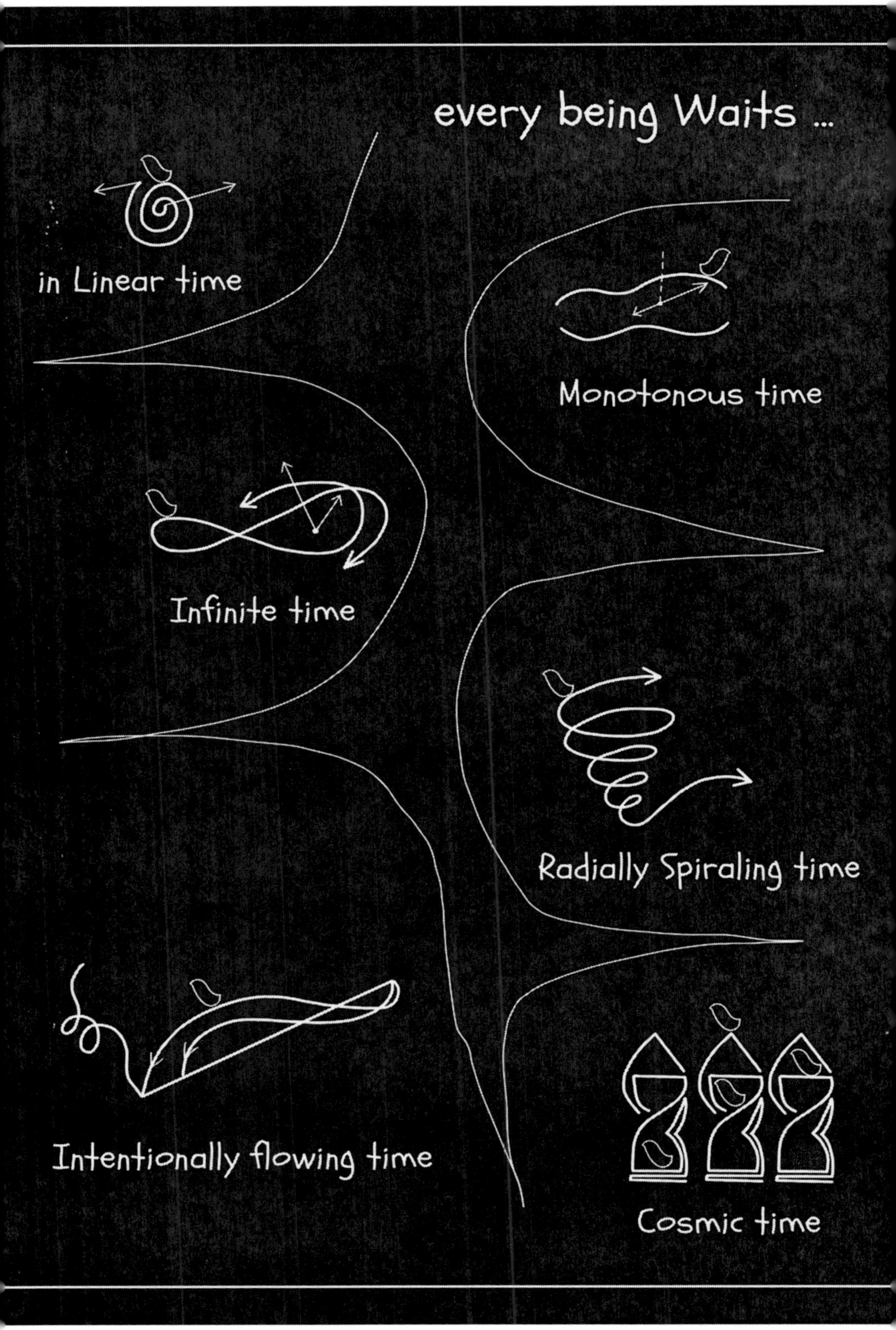
every being Waits ...
in Linear time
Monotonous time
Infinite time
Radially Spiraling time
Intentionally flowing time
Cosmic time

every being Waits every ......

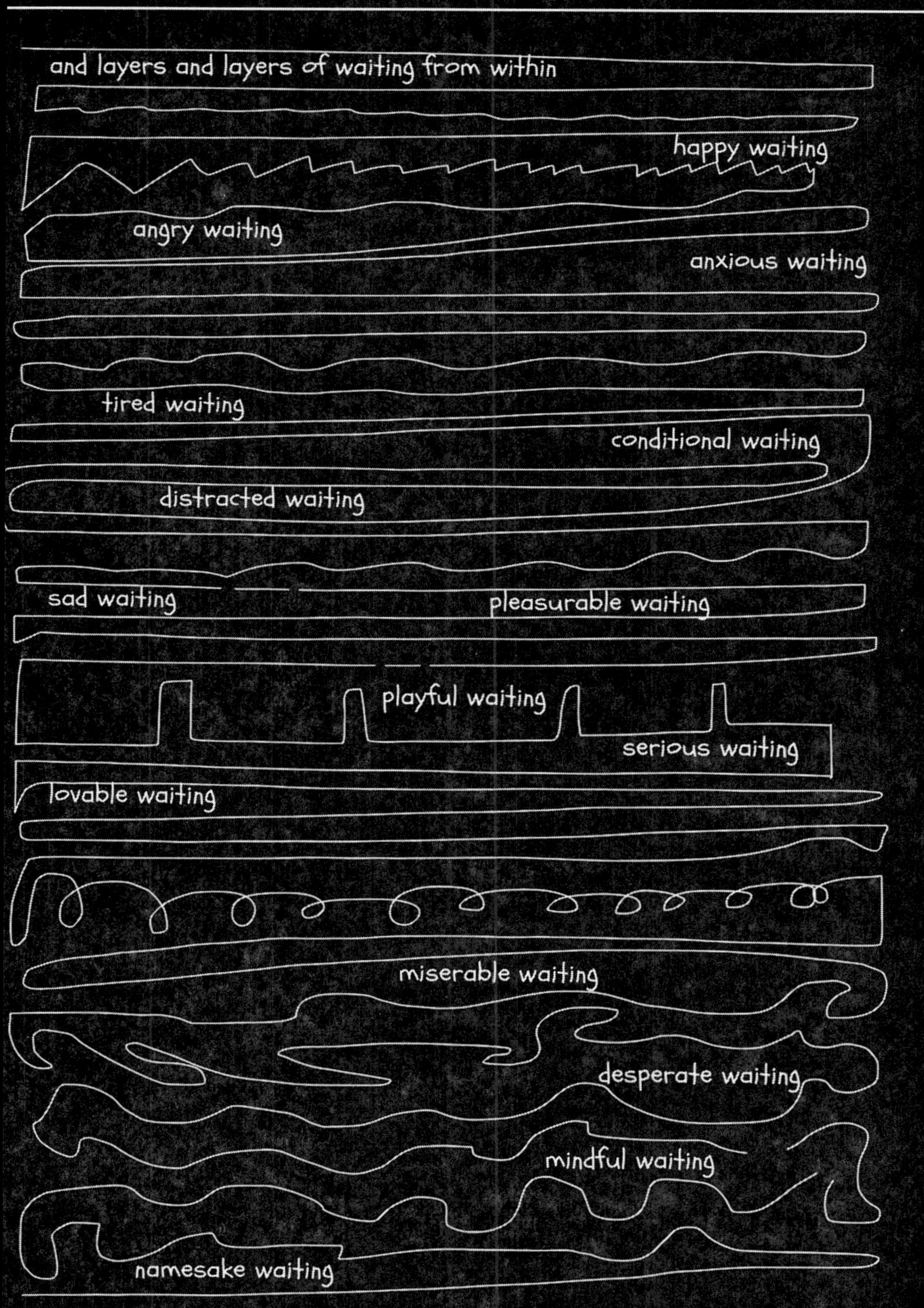
and layers and layers of waiting from within
happy waiting
angry waiting
anxious waiting
tired waiting
conditional waiting
distracted waiting
sad waiting
pleasurable waiting
playful waiting
serious waiting
lovable waiting
miserable waiting
desperate waiting
mindful waiting
namesake waiting

Once upon a Stone on a Cliff,

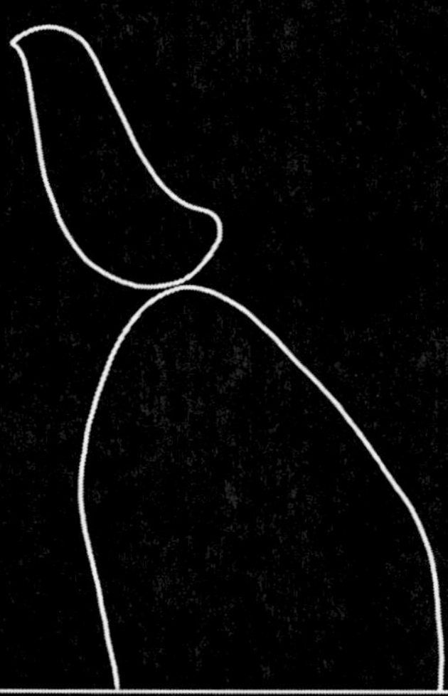

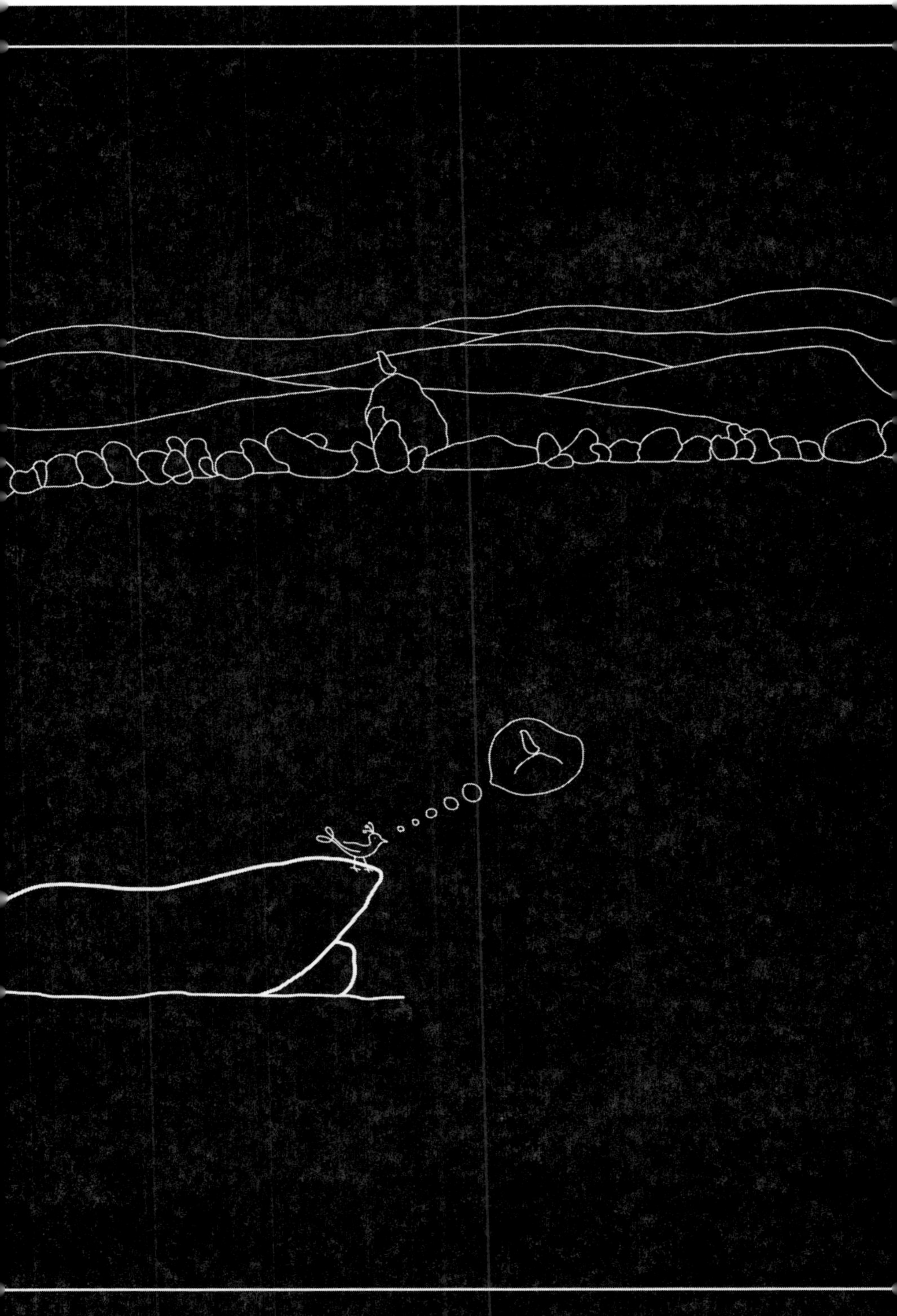

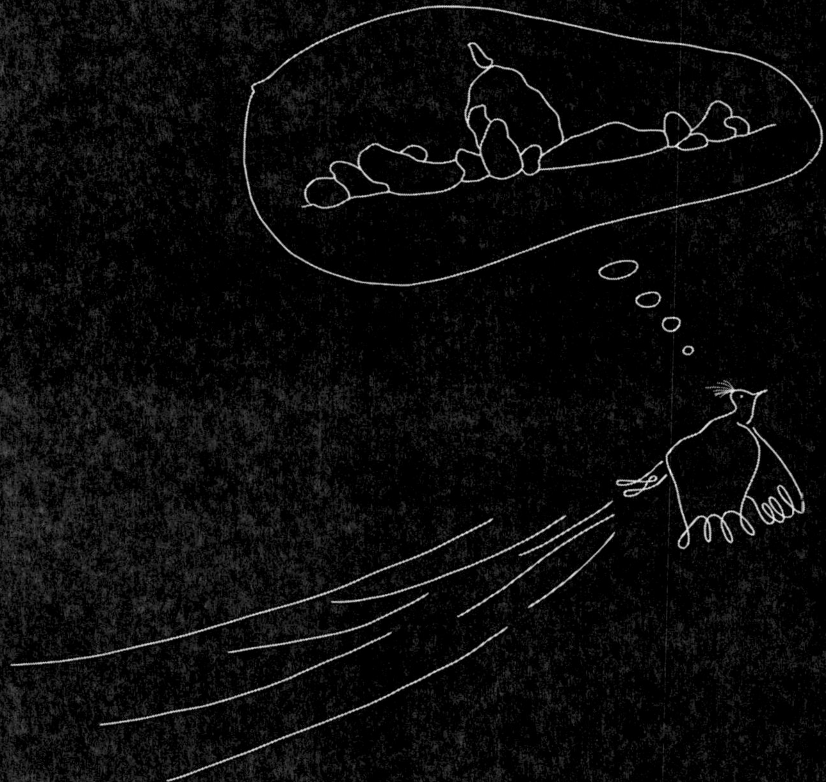

aren't you scared...?
you seem to be in a precarious position...??
won't you fall off ?

!
Truth & patience
will hold me here
until my friend comes.

i walked away from Time
..in my process of standing here for Wait to come for me.
?..

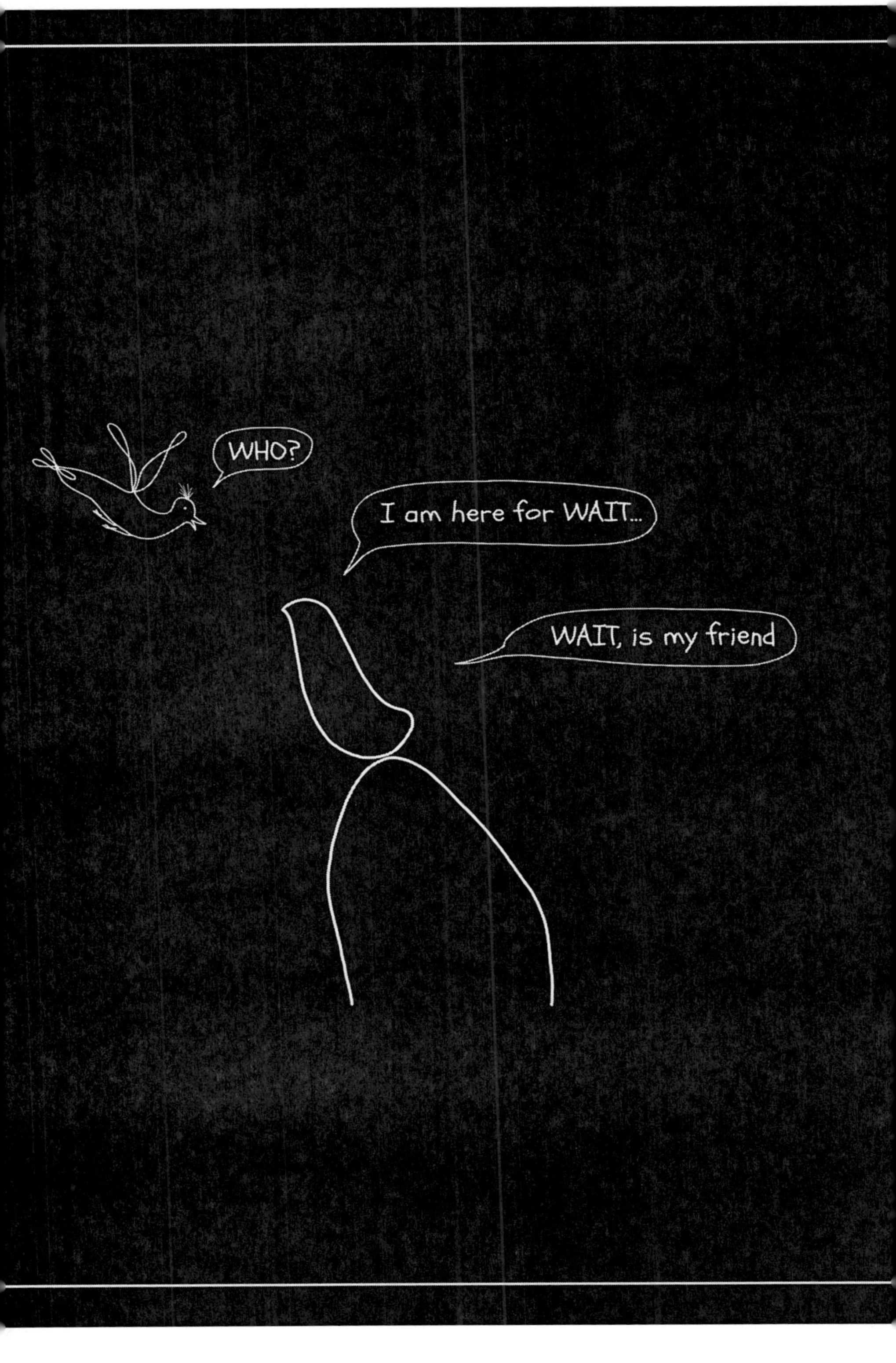
WHO?
I am here for WAIT...
WAIT, is my friend

!!!!!!
i will just 'be' until my friend 'wait' comes
then WAIT will help me grow wings and we both will fly away....

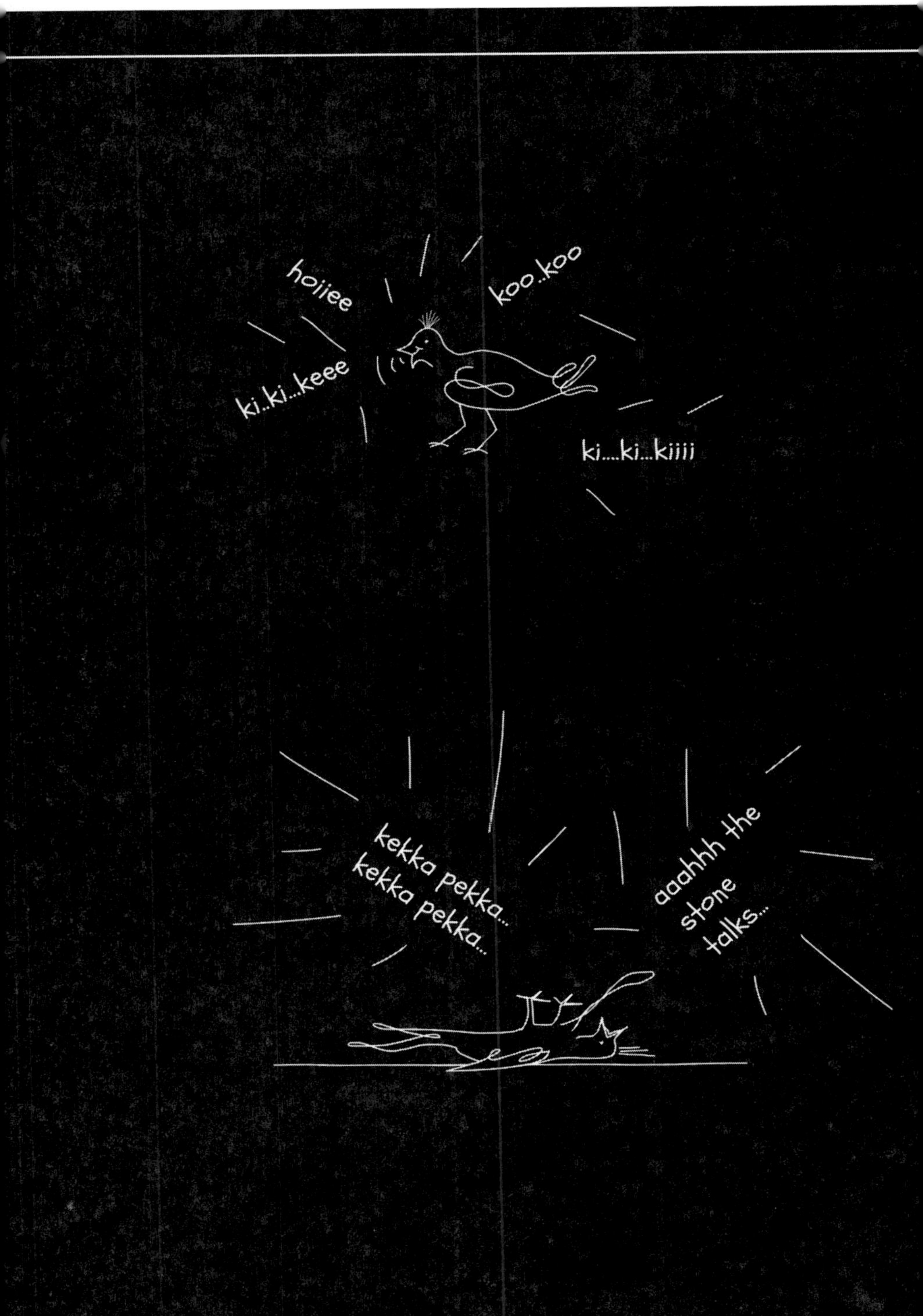
hoijiee
koo..koo
ki..ki...keee
ki....ki...kiiii
kekka pekka...
kekka pekka...
aaahhh the
stone
talks...

Sometimes the Stone would look through her mind's eyes...

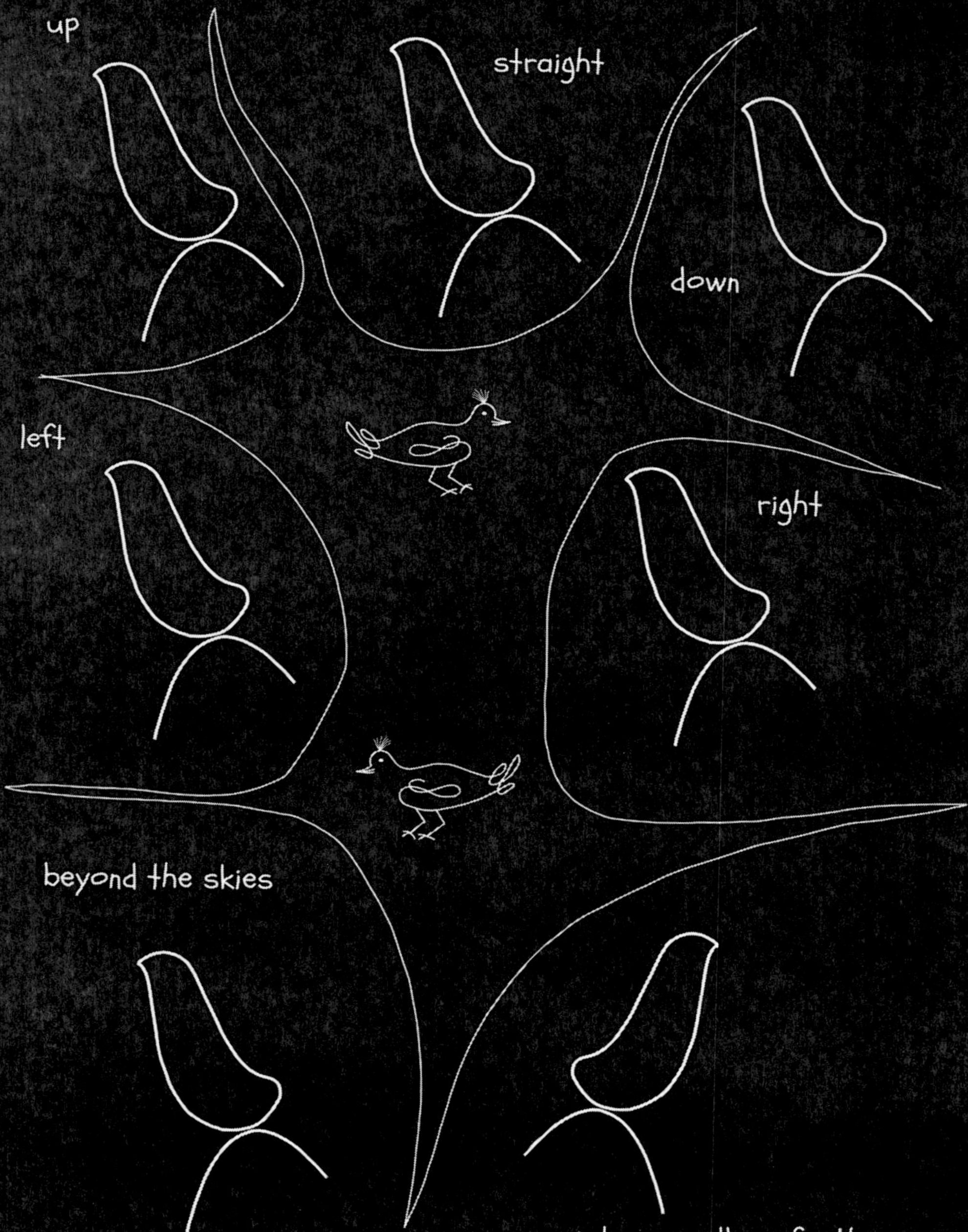

up

straight

down

left

right

beyond the skies

into an endless further...

maybe she really will fly away?
why look into an endless further?
to grow wings and fly away, she said
she just 'is'
why am i flying upside down?
who knows?

Birdoo was curious ,

and Stone was equanimous.

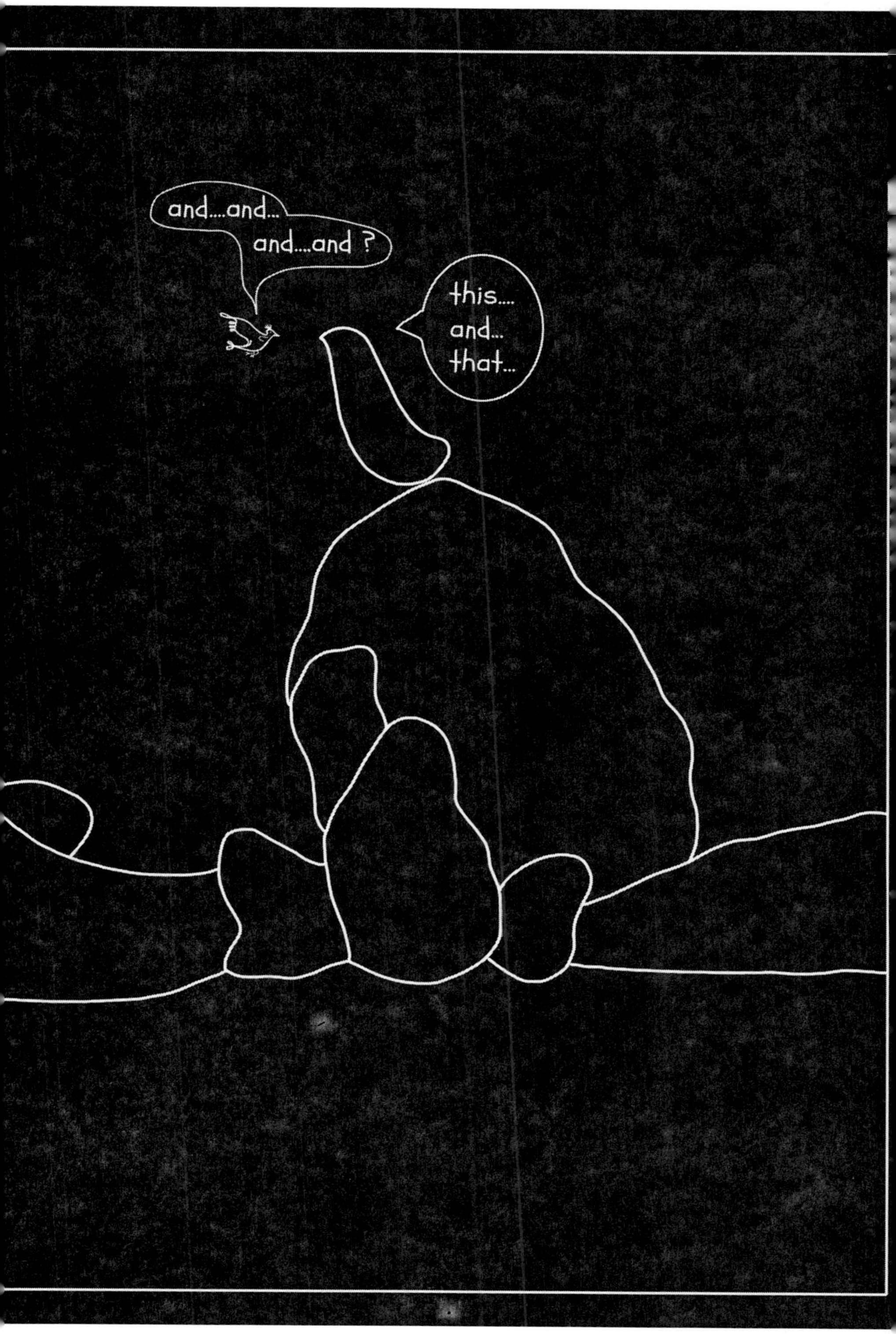
and....and...
and....and ?
this....
and...
that...

a wet spot?
what is it?

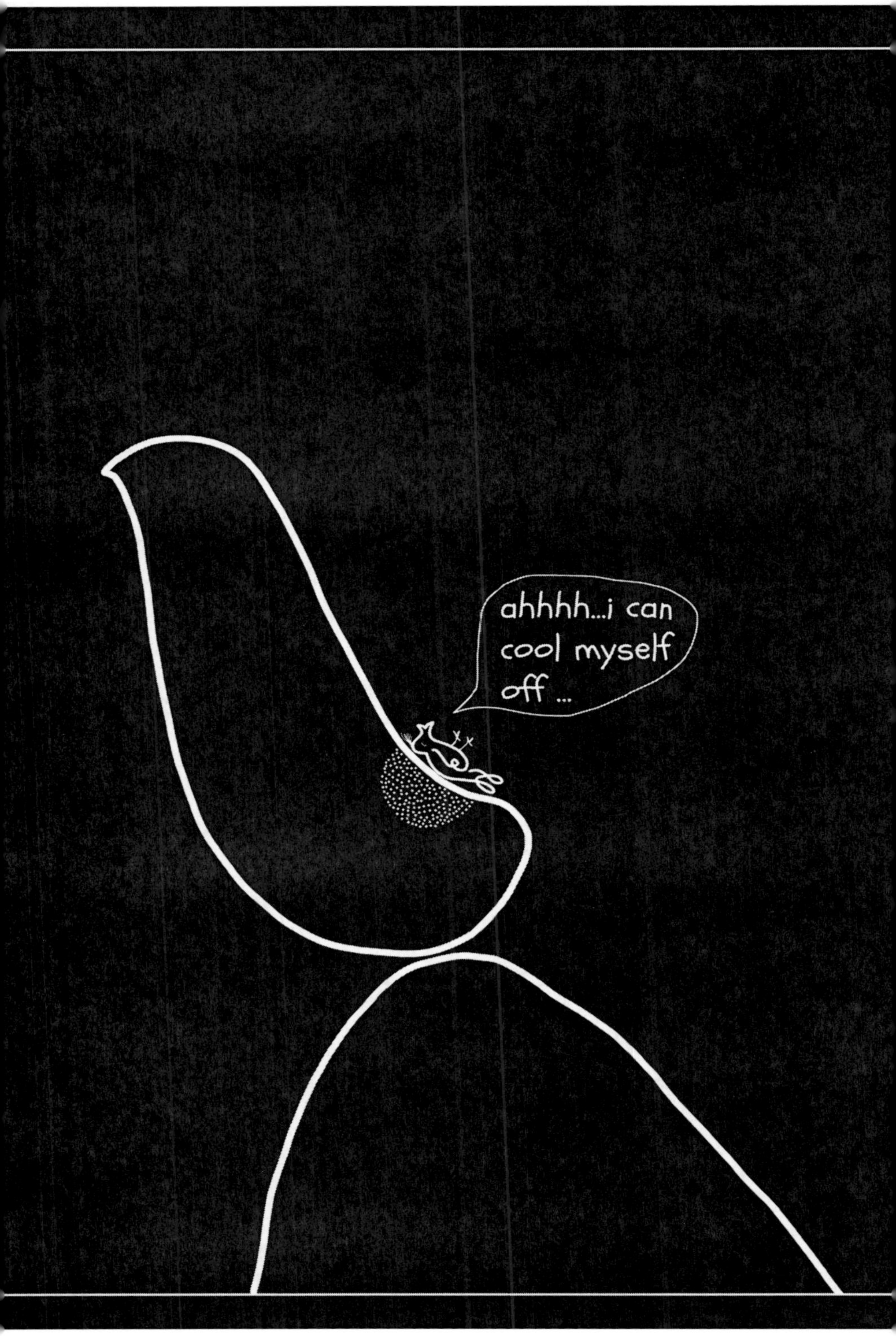
ahhhh...i can cool myself off ...

i'm ...intrigued
a talking Stone...
with a wet spot ...
what else do you hold within ???

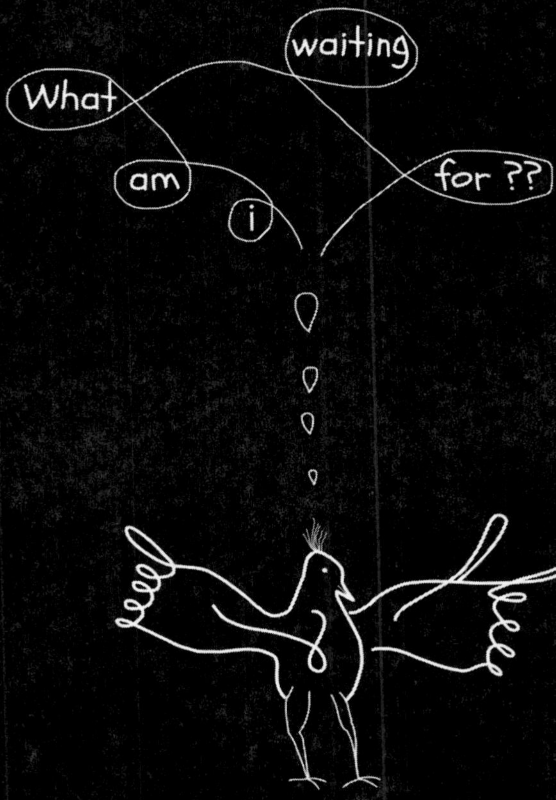
What
am
i
waiting
for ??

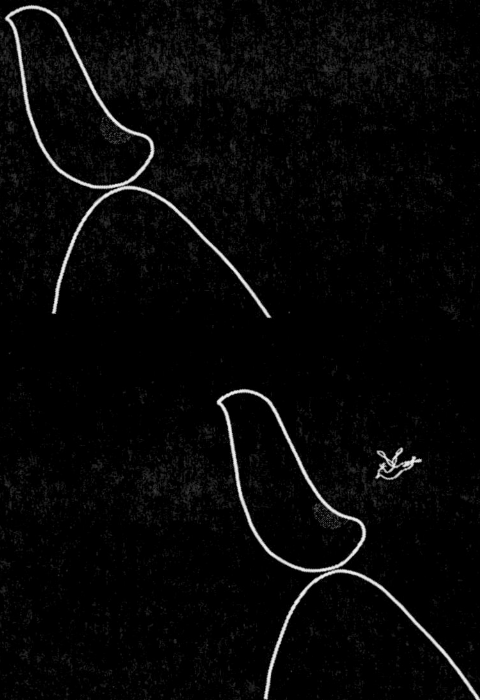

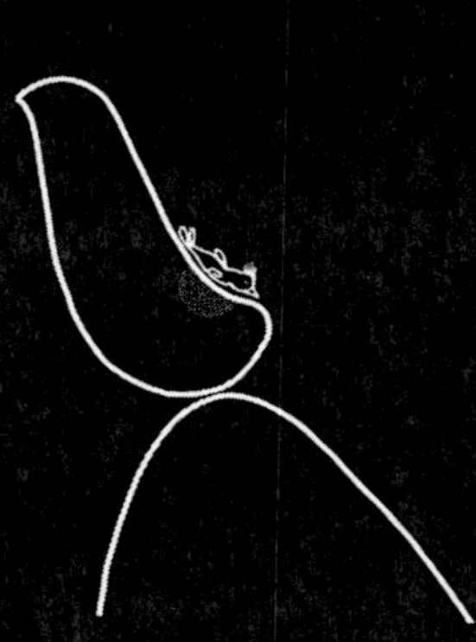

Birdoo knew how to just chill
with her new friend Stone.

A Stone Full of Wait...

Once upon a matter,

A Stone emerged from a Spiral,

And Wait appeared.

Stone and Wait enjoyed each other's company.

No words spoken.

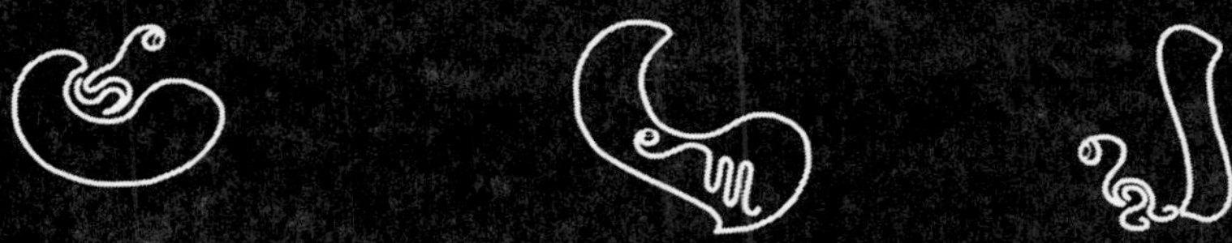

No expectations whatsoever

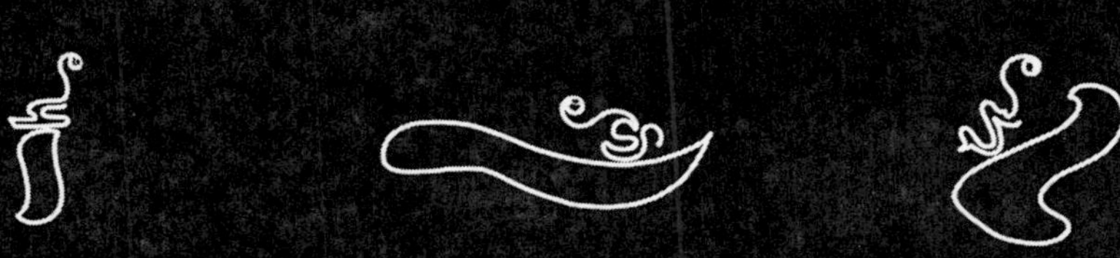

no concept of Time.

After playing around,

they would get back into the Spiral...

They appeared in and out of the Spiral.. at will...

Until,

Once, the Stone emerged...

and Wait didn't.

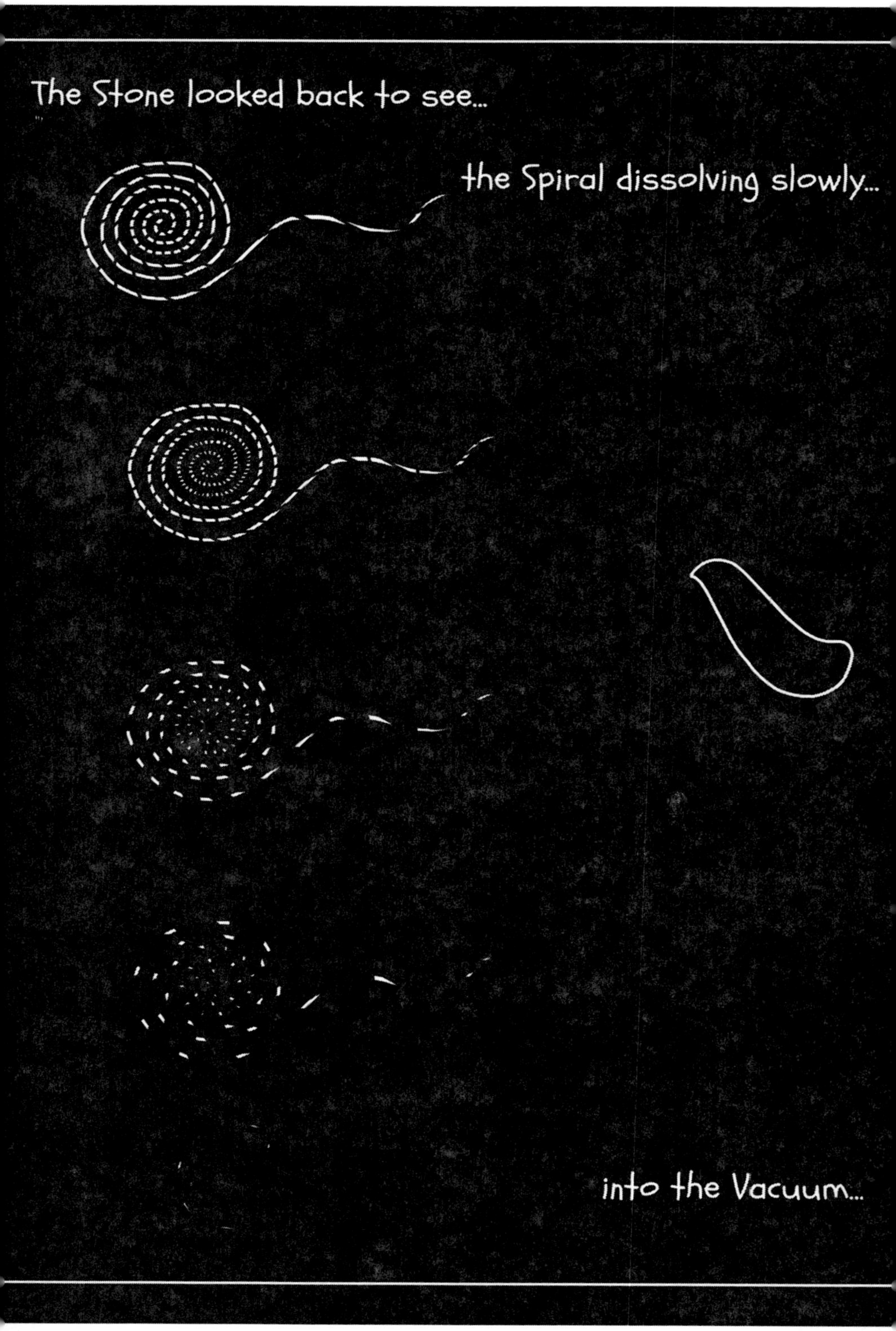
The Stone looked back to see...
the Spiral dissolving slowly...
into the Vacuum...

leaving Stone, Alone.....

.....looking for Wait...

...and the Spiral. !

Now,

there was something very special about the Stone.

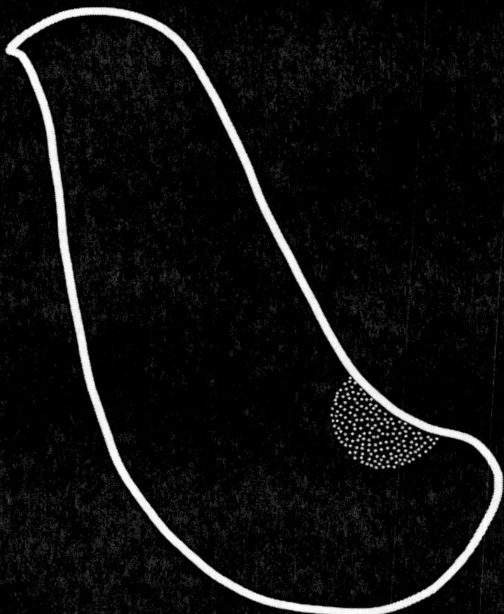

Stone had a mystery spot on her surface
which was always cool and wet.

Stone endures her existence for Wait.

Stillness....

...And Wait endures existence for Stone.

Constant change...

!!!
and...
you are
waiting for Wait??
yes

Stone Alone stood....

enduring existence...

waiting for Wait ...

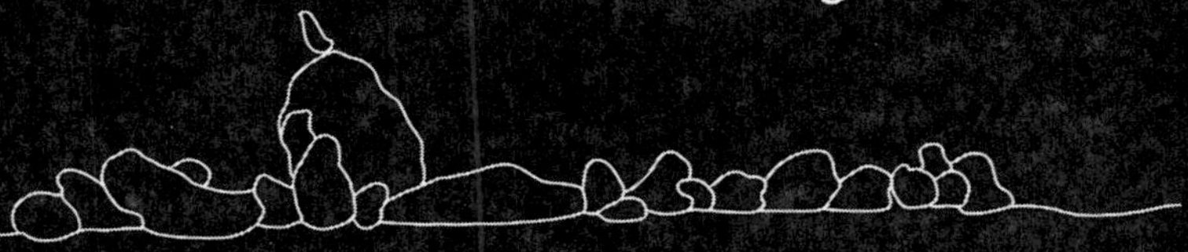

allowing other beings to rest on her...

through the passage of time

until...she moved away from time !

And , thus....

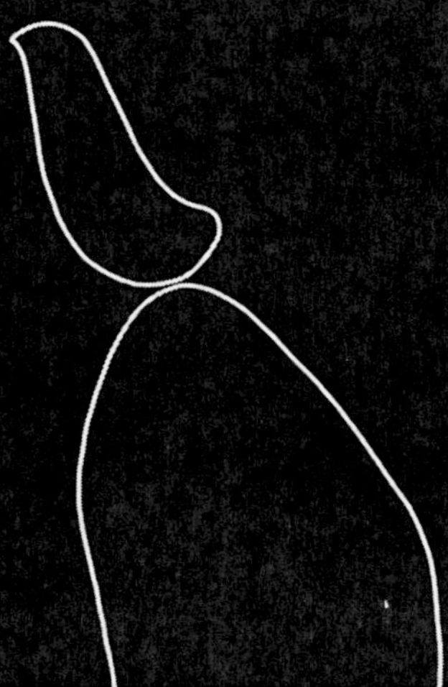

and...

and...

and...

Wait doesn't stay too long with anyone.
Wait only longs to set Stone free.

What does Wait do while waiting ?
. . . becomes one with the being that waits .

Is Wait endless?
No, Wait ends too !

Wait finds Stone...

And when Wait finally became one with Stone... ...

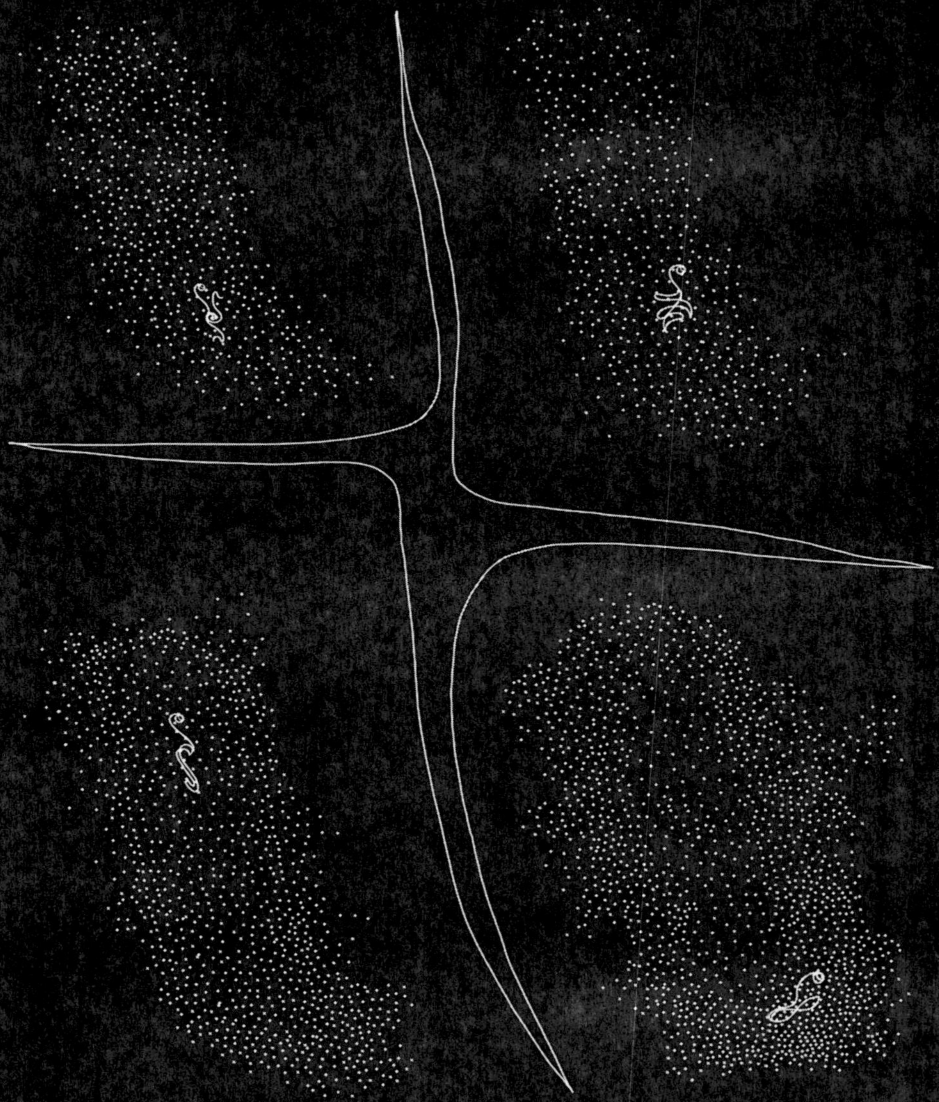

...the Stone disintegrated into infinite pieces...flying away !

Stone's secret revealed itself...

...leapt away...

leaving the Spiral behind !

Meaning of words in this story according to my understanding...

Stone - a being which silently observes while waiting.

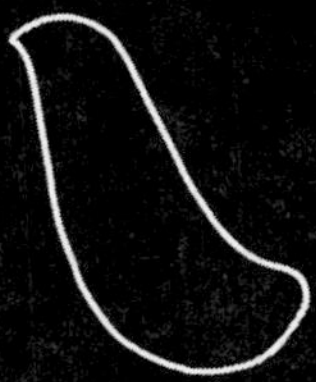

Wait - a being which patiently endures all the beings' existence

Birdoo - a being which has the option of multiple perspectives, literally

Toad - a being which is in a state of torpor in its process of waiting

...into an endless further...

epilogue

Every being holds a secret within ,
that is revealed only when its 'Wait' is fulfilled.

A Wait full of Stone

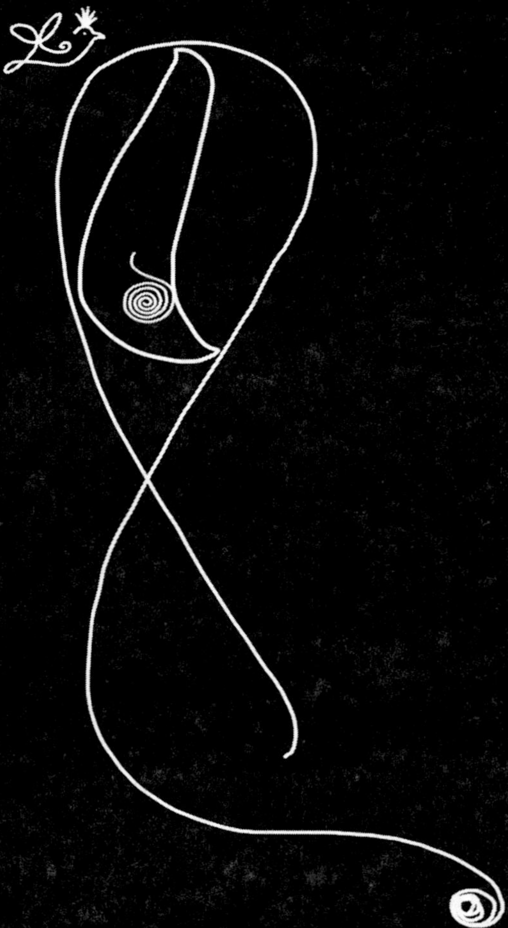

earthling k